This book belongs to

_____

Based on the TV series *Dora the Explorer*® as seen on Nick Jr.®

SIMON SPOTLIGHT
An imprint of Simon & Schuster Children's Publishing Division
1230 Avenue of the Americas, New York, New York 10020
Dora Goes to School, Dora's Book of Manners, Dora's Chilly Day, and *Dora's Fairy-Tale Adventure*
copyright © 2004 Viacom International Inc. *Big Sister Dora!, Dora's Pirate Adventure,* and
Show Me Your Smile! copyright © 2005 Viacom International Inc. All rights reserved.

NICK JR., *Dora the Explorer,* and all related titles, logos, and characters are
registered trademarks of Viacom International Inc.

NICK JR.
DORA the EXPLORER®

DORA'S
BIG BOOK
OF STORIES

Simon Spotlight
New York   London   Toronto   Sydney

Contents

It was a sunny day, and Dora and Boots were playing
hide-and-seek in the Flowery Garden.

"I found you!" shouted Dora, pointing up toward the tree.

"I've been caught!" giggled Boots.

Suddenly Dora stopped and listened. "Oh, no! I think I hear
someone crying."

Dora and Boots followed the sound over to the teary Grumpy Old Troll.

"Hi, Mr. Troll," said Dora. "Is something wrong?"

"I was very grumpy this morning, *so* grumpy that when my friend, Mouse, came over to play, I told him to go away," replied the Troll. "But now I'm sad. I wasn't very nice to Mouse and I think I hurt his feelings. Can you help me get my best friend back?"

"We can help you, Mr. Troll," replied Dora.

"Great!" said the Troll. "I know some riddles about being nice. Will you help me answer them?"

"Sure! We love riddles!" exclaimed Boots.

"All right, here's my first riddle," said the Troll.

"It was wrong to be grumpy to Mouse. I was very bad. What's the nice thing to say, so my friend won't be mad?"

"That's a great idea! I'll tell Mouse that I'm sorry!" cried the Grumpy Old Troll. "But I don't know where Mouse is," he continued sadly.

"We can check the Map," said Dora. "Say 'Map!'"

"I know how to find Mouse," said Map. "Mouse ran all the way back to his house. So you'll have to cross Sneezing Snake Lake, then go over Dragon Mountain, and that's how you'll get to Mouse's House."

Soon Dora, Boots, and the Troll arrived at the edge of Sneezing Snake Lake.

"How will we get across the lake?" wondered Boots.

Suddenly the Troll said,

"Look! It's Tico! And he's coming our way.
But how should I greet him? What's the nice thing to say?"

"Hello! *¡Hola*, Tico!" waved the Troll.
Tico offered to take Dora, Boots, and the
Troll across Sneezing Snake Lake in his boat.

They all put on life jackets and climbed aboard. Suddenly sneezing snakes started popping up!

"Achoo! Achoo!" sneezed the snakes.

"Oh, no!" said the Troll. "All this sneezing is making my nose tickle. I think I'm going to sneeze.

"I could sure use some more advice from you. When I have to sneeze, what should I do?"

Tico sailed the boat around all
the sneezing snakes.

Once they landed at the dock Dora, Boots, and the Troll jumped out of the boat.
The Troll said,

"Tico got us across the lake lickety-split!
How do we let him know we appreciate it?"

"¡*Gracias*, Tico!" called the Troll.
"¡*De nada!*" Tico replied as he sailed away.

23

"Where do we go next?" asked Boots.

"I know!" said the Troll. "We have to go over Dragon Mountain."

"Do you see anything that can take us over Dragon Mountain?" asked Boots.

24

The Troll saw an ice-cream truck driving up the road.

"Look! Our friend Val the octopus is driving that ice-cream truck. I bet she can take us over Dragon Mountain," Dora said.

"I remember what to do," said the Troll, and he called out, "*¡Hola!* Hello, Val!"

Val stopped the ice-cream truck, and they all climbed inside.

When they reached the top of Dragon Mountain, suddenly dragons jumped out and blocked the road.

"GO AWAY!" shouted the Troll.

But the dragons wouldn't budge.

"Hmm," said the Troll.

"Shouting won't scare these dragons away.
If I want them to move, what's the nice thing to say?"

"Please, dragons, will you move out of the way?" the Troll called.

"We're sorry!" the dragons replied. "We didn't mean to block the road. We just wanted some ice cream! Please? *¿Por favor?*"

"Sure!" said Val, and she handed everyone an ice-cream cone.

Suddenly they heard a rustle coming from above.

"Look, it's Swiper! He's going to try and swipe our ice cream," said Boots.

"We have to stop Swiper," said Dora. "Say 'Swiper, no swiping!'"

"Oh Mannn!" said Swiper as he flew away.

"Hmmm," said the Troll, "I just learned something:

Swiping is not a nice thing to do.
If Swiper asked nicely, he could have ice cream too!"

29

Soon Dora, Boots, and the Troll arrived at Mouse's House. The Troll knocked on the door.

"Mouse, please come out. I want to apologize," said the Troll.

Mouse opened the door and the Troll said, "I'm sorry I was grumpy. I was not a nice friend. Will you forgive me? Please? *¿Por favor?*"

Mouse was so happy to see the Troll that he said, "Yes! I forgive you!"

"Thank you! *¡Gracias!*" said the Troll.

"Hooray!" cheered Dora and Boots. "Mouse and the Troll are friends again! We did it!"

The Troll was so glad to play with his friends! He danced a happy dance as he said,

"I learned many things on our trip.
You have to be nice if you want friendship.
Friends are helpful and caring and go out of their way.
So I'll be kind and polite—at least for today!"

Dora Goes to School

adapted by Leslie Valdes
illustrated by Robert Roper

¡Hola! I'm Dora and this is my best friend, Boots. It's our first day of school today! And look, there's our teacher, *Maestra Beatriz!* She's on her way to school too.

Maestra Beatriz has to get to school before the students do, but her bicycle just got a flat tire. We have to help her get to school fast!

First she needs us to help carry her school supplies. Where can we put her supplies? Yeah! Backpack can carry them.

Now let's find the quickest way to school. Who do we ask for help when we don't know which way to go? Map, right!

Map says we need to go through Letter Town, over Number Mountain, and that's the quickest way to get to school. I hear the first school bell. We need to get to school before the third bell. We'd better hurry!

Do you see something that can take us through Letter Town fast? *Sí. El autobus* will take us through the town. *¡Vámonos!*

We need to follow the alphabet along the streets to get through Letter Town. Sing the alphabet with me!

Uh-oh, I hear the second school bell. We really need to hurry! *¡Rápido!* I see some mountains up ahead. Which one is Number Mountain?

We made it to Number Mountain! Who can give us a ride over it? Our friend Azul the train! *¡Sí!*

To ride over Number Mountain we have to count the numbers. Count with me: 1, 2, 3, 4, 5, 6, 7, 8, 9, 10. That's great!

Now let's count backward as we ride down the other side: 10, 9, 8, 7, 6, 5, 4, 3, 2, 1. Yay! We made it over Number Mountain.

There's the school! But to get there we need to cross the forest. Here comes my cousin Diego. He says the Condors can fly us over the forest.

Will you help us call the Condors so we can get to school superfast? You need to say "Squawk, squawk!" Say it louder!

Good calling!
Now we can ride the Condors all the way to the school.
You need to hold on tight! Whee!

We made it to school! Now we have to run inside and set up the classroom before the other students come in.

Will you check Backpack to find *Maestra Beatriz's* school supplies?

Yay! We found *Maestra Beatriz's* school supplies, but I hear Swiper! That sneaky fox will try to swipe them! We have to say "Swiper, no swiping!" Say it with me: "Swiper, no swiping!"

Thanks for helping us stop Swiper! Look, here come *Maestra Beatriz's* other students.

"Good morning, class!" says *Maestra Beatriz.*

"*¡Buenos dias!*" say the students.

I hear the third school bell! Thanks for helping us get to school on time!

Dora's Fairy-Tale Adventure

adapted by Christine Ricci
illustrated by Susan Hall

Once upon a time....

Dora and Boots were playing in Fairy-Tale Land.
    Suddenly when Boots wasn't looking, a mean witch cast a spell and turned him into Sleeping Boots! The people of Fairy-Tale Land told Dora that the only thing that could wake Boots was a hug from a true princess.

Dora was worried. She didn't know any true princesses. "I have an idea!" exclaimed a friendly dwarf. "*You* can become a true princess and wake up Sleeping Boots."

The dwarfs told Dora that in order to become a true princess she had to pass four tests. First she had to find the red ring. Then she had to teach the Giant Rocks to sing. Then she had to turn winter into spring. And finally she had to bring the moon to the Queen and King.

Dora immediately set off to find the red ring. But it was hidden in a dark and scary cave. Dora didn't want to wake the Dragon who lived in the cave, so she quietly tiptoed inside. There she spotted the glow of the red ring.

But just as Dora reached for the ring, the Dragon awoke!

Dora quickly slipped the ring onto her finger. In a flash the Dragon's cave turned into a beautiful palace. And the Dragon was transformed into a prince!

The Prince told Dora that the Mean Witch had turned him into a dragon. He was so grateful to Dora for setting him free that he gave Dora a magic music box.

"This will help you become a true princess," said the Prince.

Dora thanked him and started down the path toward her next test.

Soon Dora came upon the Giant Rocks.

"How can I teach these Giant Rocks to sing?" she wondered. Then Dora remembered the magic music box that the Prince had given her. She carefully turned the handle.

The music box started to play the most wonderful tune. The music was so delightful that Dora was sure it would make anyone sing and dance.

"*Boingy, boingy, boingy, bing. We'll get these rocks to sing!*" sang the magic music box.

Slowly the Giant Rocks opened their eyes. And then, to Dora's amazement, they began to dance and sing!

"Boingy, boingy, boingy, bing. You've taught us how to sing!"

When the song was over, Dora told the rocks that she had
to be on her way.

"Sleeping Boots needs my help!" she said.

"Wait!" exclaimed the Giant Rocks as they gave Dora a
present. "Here's a little bag of sunshine to help you become
a true princess."

Dora thanked the Giant Rocks and ran down the path.

Soon Dora started to feel cold. Snow began to fall and a chilly wind whirled all around her.

"I must be in Winter Valley," she thought. "How will I turn winter into spring?"

Suddenly she remembered the little bag of sunshine. Dora opened the bag, and a small sun floated up into the sky.

The sun's rays melted all the snow. Flowers bloomed. Leaves grew on the trees. Birds, butterflies, and animals came out to play in the soft new grass.

"Thanks for turning winter into spring," said the animals.

"Take this magic hairbrush," said a little rabbit. "It will help you become a true princess so you can wake up Sleeping Boots."

At last Dora came upon a castle. She climbed the stairs to the top of a high tower. Now Dora faced the hardest test of all.

"How am I going to bring the moon to the Queen and King?" she wondered.

Dora looked up at the moon and knew that she was going to need some help from her friends.

Isa, Tico, and Benny heard Dora's call for help. But before they could reach her, the Mean Witch made the stairs to the tower disappear. Then Dora had a wonderful idea. She took out the magic hairbrush and began to brush her hair. With each stroke her hair grew longer until it hung all the way down to the ground.

Dora called down to her friends. "Come on! Climb up my hair!"

Dora asked Isa, Tico, and Benny to help her figure out a way to get to the moon. The friends thought hard, and soon they had a plan: They called to the stars!

The stars twinkled and glowed as they flew down from the sky. Then they made a staircase that led all the way to the moon!

Dora climbed and climbed until she reached the moon.

"*Hola*, Dora!" said the moon. "How can I help you?"

"Moon," said Dora, "I need you to visit the Queen and King."

When the moon heard about Sleeping Boots, he agreed to help her and floated down to the tower.

"Dora," said the King. "You have found the red ring. You have taught the Giant Rocks to sing. You have turned winter into spring. And you have brought the moon to the Queen and King. You are now a true princess!"

The moon glowed in the sky. The stars twinkled. And rainbows danced through the air as Dora magically turned into a true princess!

"Hooray for Princess Dora!" everyone cheered.

The King's unicorns flew Princess Dora all the way back to Sleeping Boots.

Princess Dora wrapped her arms around Sleeping Boots
and gave him the biggest hug ever! And then . . . Sleeping
Boots opened his eyes!

83

And so Sleeping Boots awoke at last. The Mean Witch flew far, far away and was never seen again. And everyone in Fairy-Tale Land lived happily every after!

The End

Dora's Chilly Day

by Kiki Thorpe
illustrated by Steven Savitsky

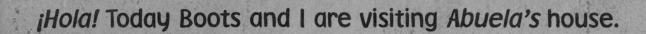

¡*Hola!* Today Boots and I are visiting *Abuela's* house.

Brrr! It's chilly today. *Abuela* is going to make a chilly day surprise! She needs milk, sugar, and chocolate . . .

Uh-oh! *Abuela* has run out of chocolate. She can't make the surprise without it!

LECHE

MILK

Wait! I know where we can get some: the Chocolate Tree! Boots and I will go to the Chocolate Tree to get some chocolate for *Abuela*. Will you help us? Great!

First we'll need something to help us stay warm outside. Let's look in Backpack. Say "Backpack!"

Do you see something that will keep us warm? Right! Some mittens and hats will help us stay warm! Now we're ready to go and see our friend the Chocolate Tree.

Let's ask Map what the best way is to the Chocolate Tree.

Map says that to get to the Chocolate Tree we have to go over the Troll Bridge and through the Nutty Forest. *¡Vámonos!* Let's go!

Brrr! The wind sure is strong. What a chilly day!
Look, there's Diego. I wonder what Diego likes to do on a chilly day . . .

Diego is bringing some straw to Mama Blue Bird so she can build a nice warm nest for her Blue Bird babies. Nice work, Diego! Come on! We're almost at the Troll Bridge.

We made it to the Troll Bridge. And there's the Grumpy Old Troll. What do you think the Grumpy Old Troll likes to do on a chilly day?

The Grumpy Old Troll likes to make up new riddles! And he has a special chilly day riddle for us:

"This riddle is tricky. You'll have to think twice. When water freezes, it turns into . . ."

That's a hard one. Do you know the answer?

Ice, right! Yay! We solved the Troll's riddle. Now we can cross the Troll Bridge!

Look! There's our friend the Big Red Chicken. I wonder what the Big Red Chicken likes to do on a chilly day . . .

The Big Red Chicken is knitting a big red scarf! That will help him stay nice and warm.

Do you remember where we go next? That's right— the Nutty Forest! *Adiós,* Big Red Chicken!

Uh-oh. That's a very mucky mud puddle. We have to cross it to get to the Nutty Forest. Do you see a way to get to the other side?

We can use those stepping-stones.
Good thinking!

Mmmm! What's that delicious smell? It's coming from Tico's Tree House!

Tico likes to bake Nutty Butter Cookies on a chilly day. And he has some cookies for us! *Gracias*, Tico. Come on, let's hurry. We're almost there!

We made it! *Hola,* Chocolate Tree! *Abuela* needs three pieces of chocolate for her surprise. Do you see three pieces?

I can't wait to see what the chilly day surprise is. Let's hurry back to *Abuela's* house. Remember to keep an eye out for Swiper. That sneaky fox will try to swipe our chocolate. If you see him, say "Swiper, no swiping!"

107

Hooray! We brought the chocolate home to *Abuela.* Now she can make the chilly day surprise.

Abuela taught us a special chocolate song in Spanish. While *Abuela* mixes in the chocolate, we can help her by singing. Will you sing with us? Great!

¡Bate, bate—chocolate!
¡Bate, bate—chocolate!

Abuela's chilly day surprise is hot chocolate. ¡Delicioso! I love drinking hot chocolate on a chilly day.
What do *you* like to do on a chilly day?

Show Me Your Smile!

A Visit to the Dentist

by Christine Ricci
illustrated by Robert Roper

¡Hola! I'm Dora! I'm going to the dentist's office to have my teeth cleaned today. Have you ever been to the dentist?

I have to wait for my turn with the dentist. The waiting room has lots of things to do. I want to color a picture. Do you see some crayons?

crayons

The dental assistant is calling my name. It's my turn! Will you come with me into the dentist's office? Great! Let's go! *¡Vámonos!*

Wow! Look at all the neat things! There's a big chair that goes up and down. Do you see a light? The dentist needs a light to see inside my mouth. What else do you see in the dentist's room?

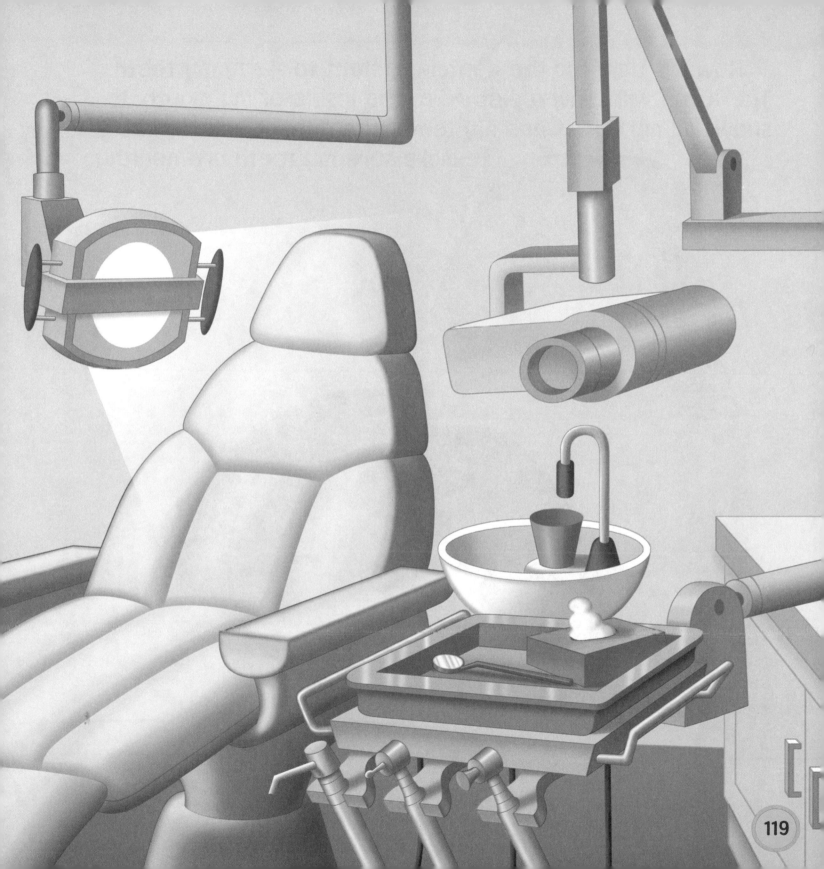

Now it's time for the dental assistant to X-ray my teeth. The X ray will show a picture of the inside of my mouth. It shows all my bones and my teeth. The dentist can look at it to make sure my teeth are healthy.

The dental assistant covers me with a heavy apron. Then I have to sit very still for the camera. When the camera goes *click*, the X ray is done!

Can you find the X ray of my teeth? Who else had their teeth X-rayed at the dentist's office?

Here comes the dentist! She uses special tools to check and clean my teeth.

Do you see the tool with a circle on the end of it? It's a mirror for your mouth! The dentist uses it to see all the hidden areas around your teeth. The tool with a hook on the end is called an *explorer*. The dentist uses it to explore your teeth. Hey, the dentist is an explorer just like me!

I need to open my mouth really wide, so the dentist can check my teeth. Can you open your mouth really wide? Great! Open wide! *¡Abre!*

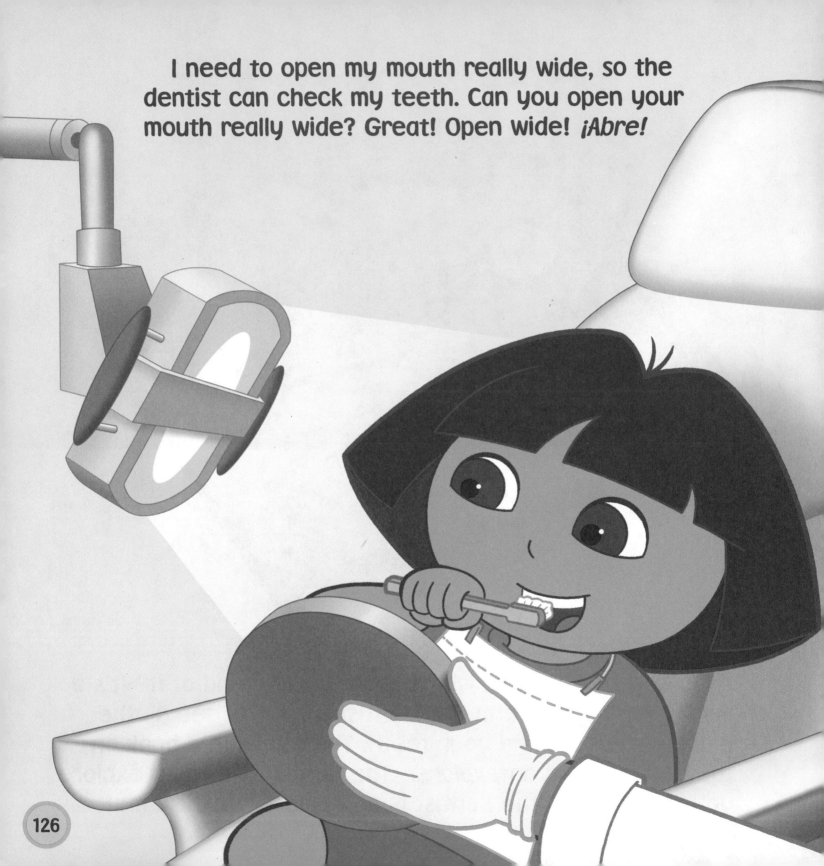

First the dentist cleaned my teeth with a special tool. Now she is showing me how to brush my teeth with a toothbrush. The dentist says I should brush after breakfast and again before bedtime.

Time to floss my teeth! The dentist takes a long piece of waxy string called dental floss and wiggles it between my teeth. She says that I should have my *mami* help me floss every night to make sure that the spaces between my teeth stay clean.

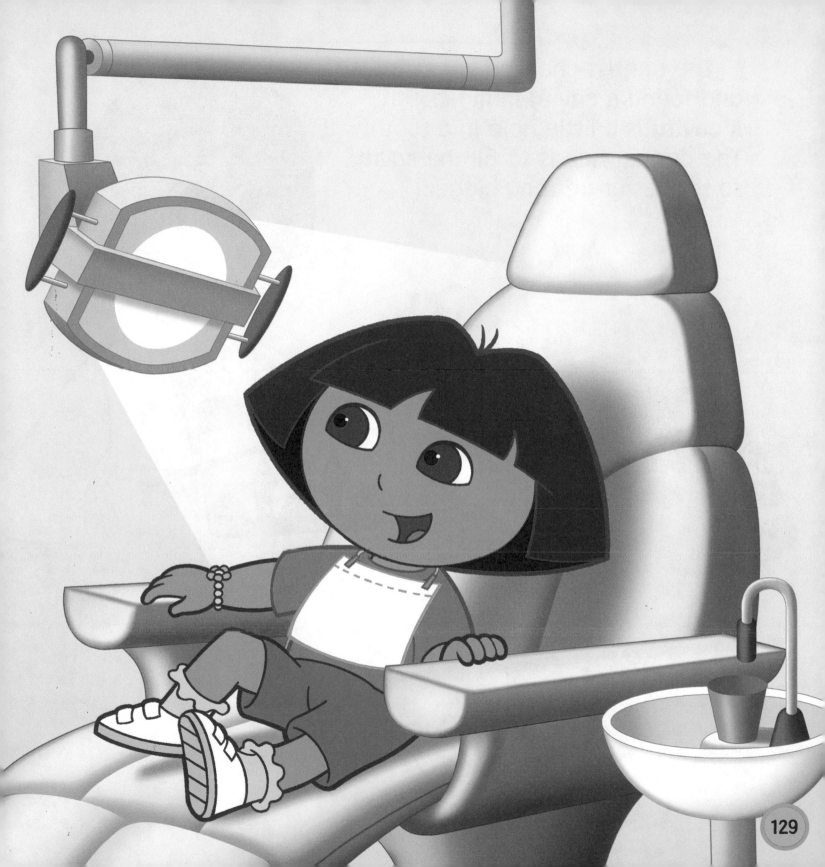

The dentist checked my X ray
and found a cavity in my mouth.
A cavity is a little hole in a tooth.
The dentist needs to fill the cavity,
so it doesn't get any bigger.

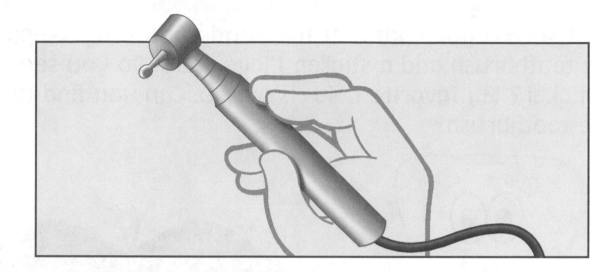

She uses a tool to get my tooth ready for the filling. It makes a funny *whirrrrring* sound as it spins around and around. Then the dentist fills the hole. Now my tooth is all better! All my teeth feel shiny and new!

I was such a good patient! The dentist is letting me pick out a new toothbrush and a sticker. I love stars! Do you see the star sticker? My favorite color is purple. Can you find the purple toothbrush?

FOR OUR BEST PATIENTS!

PICK 1

Oh, no! I hear Swiper the fox! He'll try to swipe the stickers and toothbrushes. If you see Swiper, say "Swiper, no swiping!"

Yay! We stopped Swiper.

Swiper will get his very own sticker and toothbrush after the dentist cleans his teeth!

¡Excelente! Now I have bright, clean, shiny teeth.
Going to the dentist makes me want to SMILE!
Show me your smile!
Good smiling! We did it!

Dora's Pirate Adventure

by Leslie Valdes

illustrated by Dave Aikins

Ahoy, mateys! I'm Dora. Do you want to be in our pirate play?
Great! Let's go put on our costumes!

Uh-oh. That sounds like pirates. Do you see pirates?

The Pirate Piggies are taking our costume chest! They think it's full of treasure.

If we don't get the costumes back, we can't dress up like pirates. And if we can't dress up like pirates, then we can't put on our pirate play.

We can get our costumes back. We just have to know where to go. Who do we ask for help when we don't know where to go? The Map!

Map says the Pirate Piggies took the treasure chest to Treasure Island. We have to sail across the Seven Seas and go under the Singing Bridge, and that's how we'll get to Treasure Island.

Do you see the Seven Seas? Yeah, there they are!
We can use that boat to sail across!

¡Fantástico! Now it's time to sail the Seven Seas. Let's count the Seven Seas together. *Uno, dos, tres, cuatro, cinco, seis, siete.*

Good counting!
Now we need to find the Singing
Bridge. Where is the bridge?

Yeah, there it is. ¡Vámonos!

The Singing Bridge sings silly songs.

Row, row, row your boat,
Gently down the stream,
Merrily, merrily,
merrily, merrily,
Life is but a
bowl of spaghetti!

We have to teach him the right words.
Let's sing the song the right way.

Row, row, row your boat,
Gently down the stream,
Merrily, merrily, merrily, merrily,
Life is but a dream!

Yay! We made it past the Singing Bridge! Next up is Treasure Island. Do you see Treasure Island? Yeah, there it is!

Look! There's a waterfall. Isa has to turn the wheel, or we'll go over the edge.

Uh-oh! The wheel broke! Maybe Backpack has something that will help us. Quick, say "Backpack!"

We need something to fix the wheel. Do you see the sticky tape?
Yeah, there it is! *¡Muy bien!*

Turn the wheel, Isa!
Whew! We made it past the waterfall.
Come on! Let's go to Treasure Island, and get our costumes back!

We found Treasure Island. Now let's look for the treasure chest. We can use Diego's spotting scope.

There it is! Come on, mateys, let's go get our costumes back!

The Pirate Piggies say they won't give us back our treasure.
We need your help. When I count to three, you need to say
"Give us back our treasure!" Ready? One, two, three:
Give us back our treasure!

It worked! *¡Muy bien!* The Pirate Piggies say we can have our treasure chest back!

Thanks for helping us get our costumes back. Now we can put on our pirate play. We did it! Hurray!

Big Sister Dora!

adapted by Alison Inches
illustrated by Dave Aikins

¡Hola! I'm Dora and this is Boots. Today I have really exciting news. Someone new is going to join my family! It's someone who sleeps in a cradle, drinks from a bottle, wears diapers, and likes to be rocked to sleep! Can you guess who it is?

A baby! *¡Sí!* My *mami* is going to have a baby! Boots says I'm going to be a great big sister. And he's going to teach the baby to do the Monkey Dance! Let's hurry home—the baby is coming right now! We need to find the quickest way to my house.

Map says first we have to go through the Spooky Forest. Then we have to go through the Nut Farm. And that's how we'll get to my house. Hurry! My *mami's* having a baby!

Look! It's the Spooky Forest. And there's Isa the iguana. Isa! Isa! My *mami's* having a baby! I'm going to be a great big sister, Boots will teach the baby the Monkey Dance, . . . and you can teach the baby about flowers, plants, and butterflies.

There are lots of spooky animals in the Spooky Forest, like snakes and crocodiles.

We need to take the path with the Friendly Frog. Should we take the first path, the second path, or the third path?

The third path! Right! Smart looking! We made it through the Spooky Forest. Next we need to go to the Nut Farm. Do you see the Nut Farm? I see it too! And there's our friend Benny the bull.

Benny! Benny! My *mami's* having a baby! I'm going to be a great big sister, Boots will teach the baby the Monkey Dance, Isa can teach the baby about flowers, plants, and butterflies, . . . and you can give the baby piggyback rides.

175

The Nut Farm is far away, but Benny says he will drive us if we can help him put the tires on his go-cart. Let's count the tires in Spanish. *Uno, dos, tres, cuatro.*

We made it to the Nut Farm! And there's our friend Tico with his cousins!

Tico! Tico! *¡Mi mami va a tener un bebé!* My *mami's* having a baby!

Tico says he can teach the baby how to speak Spanish. *Gracias,* Tico!

Map says we need to go to my house next. Do you see my house? There it is! Come on! We have to get home quickly. My *mami's* having a baby!

Look! My whole family is here! They are wearing *capias*, special pins to celebrate the baby. My *papi* says the baby is here too—that means I'm a big sister!

My *papi* also says he has an even bigger surprise. What can it be?

Twins! My *mami* had two babies. I have a baby brother *and* a baby sister.

¡Hola! I'm your big sister, Dora. Someday you'll go exploring with me!

Look! The babies smiled at me!

My *mami* says the babies are tired. We need to rock them to sleep. Will you make a cradle with your arms and help rock the babies to sleep?

Great rocking! The babies are asleep.

We did it! *¡Lo hicimos!* Thanks for helping me get home
quickly to see my new baby brother and sister!

Say it in Spanish!

abre	open	AH-bray
abuela	grandmother	ah-BWEH-lah
adiós	good-bye	ah-dee-OHS
azul	blue	ah-SOOL
bate	mix	BAH-tay
buenos días	good morning	BWEH-nohs DEE-ahs
cinco	five	SIN-koh
cuatro	four	KWAH-troh
de nada	It's nothing/You're welcome	deh NAH-dah
delicioso	delicious	deh-lee-see-OH-soh
dos	two	dohs
el autobús	the bus	el ow-toh-BOOS
excelente	excellent	ex-seh-LEN-tay
fantástico	fantastic	fahn-TAHS-tee-koh
gracias	thanks	GRAH-see-ahs
hola	hello	OH-lah